# Granddad's Story

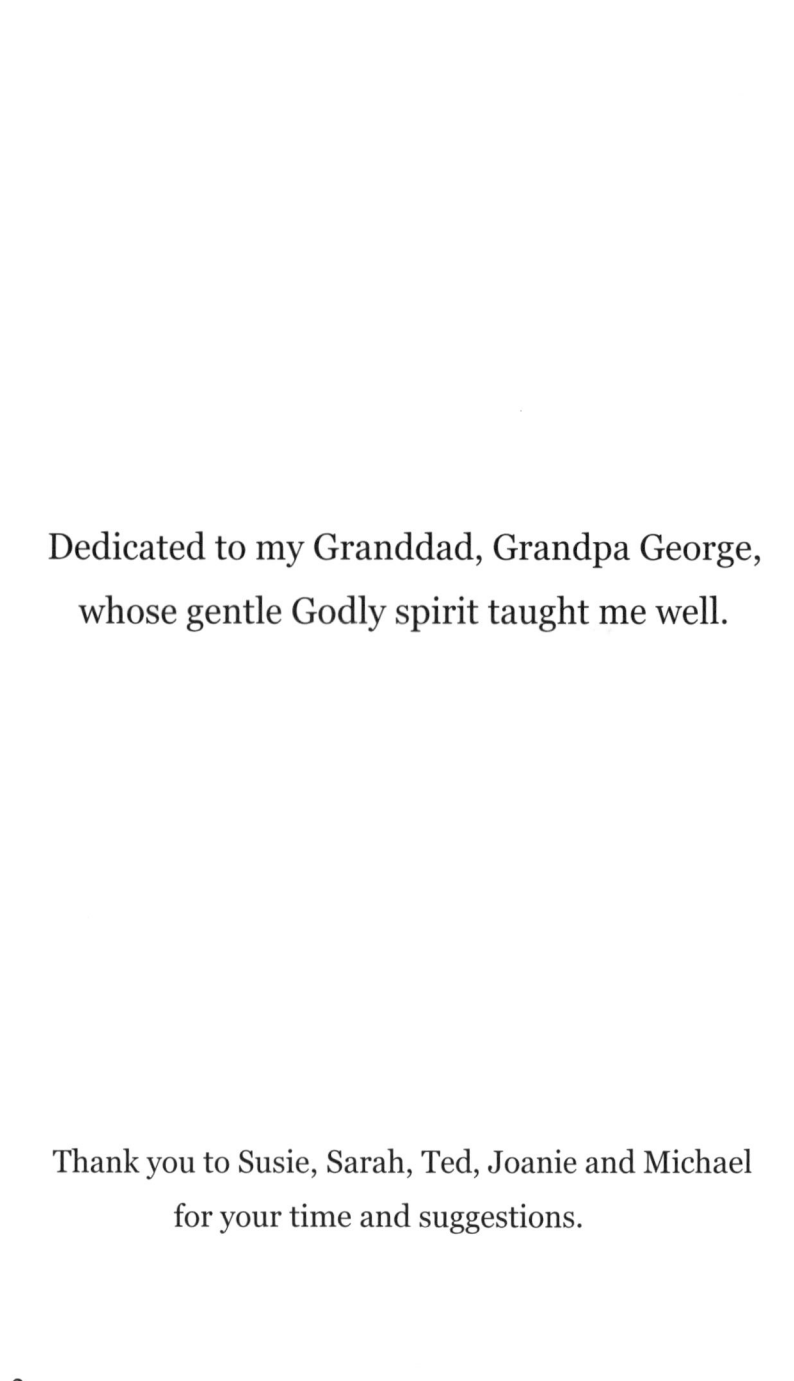

Dedicated to my Granddad, Grandpa George, whose gentle Godly spirit taught me well.

Thank you to Susie, Sarah, Ted, Joanie and Michael for your time and suggestions.

Granddad's Story
Copyright 2015 Roger Deloach

All rights reserved. This book may not be reproduced or quoted in whole or part without written permission from the publisher.

Published by:
CDM Productions
P.O. Box 161401
Duluth, MN. 55816
cdmproductions.net

Printed in the United States of America
Granddad's Story

First Edition
10 9 8 7 6 5 4 3 2 1

ISBN: 978-0-692-55983-3
Fiction

Scripture quotations taken from the New American Standard Bible, Copyright 1960, 1962, 1963, 1968, 1971, 1972, 1973, 1975, 1977, 1995 by The Lockman Foundation - Used by permission. (www.Lockman.org)

Cover Illustrations By Sue Deloach

GRANDDAD'S STORY

# Chapter 1

"Emmeline." Em's mom doesn't yell; she changes tone. Each tone has its own meaning and this one means eleven year old Emmeline neglected to do what she was asked.

"Yes, mom?"

"I asked you to finish clearing the table."

Emmeline twisted her head around to see her apron clad mom standing in the kitchen doorway. "Could I please do it later? Granddad is going to tell us a story."

"I would like to finish doing the dishes. Granddad will be more than happy to wait for you. Won't you, Granddad?"

Emmeline begged through her eyes as she turned back to the elderly man who was leaning forward in his wingback chair.

"Of course I'll wait." The old man was in no hurry. He added with a wink, "Nothing wrong with a little anticipation." Granddad smiled at the grandchildren in front of him. Kadin, Josiah and Caleb, all two years younger than their cousin Emmeline, were sitting on the floor with backs straight and legs crossed. It wouldn't be long before that stiff posture would give way to a comfortable sprawl. Noelle and Lydia were playing blocks with baby Addy. These girl cousins were three years older than the toddler, which gave them the opportunity to be the teachers instead of the students. Devyn was the oldest, the first grandchild to enter the teen years. He sat on the couch. The two youngest, Katelyn and Raya, were asleep in their cribs, unaware of the tales yet to be told. "It'll give Grandma time to make popcorn for this bunch," Granddad said. "You never know how long a story might take."

The twinkle in Granddad's eye left Emmeline guessing if the story they were about to hear was true, or another tall tale from the man they loved to listen to. With a small bowl of popcorn embellished with sliced apples and caramel dip from Grandma's hand now in front of each child, Granddad set the stage.
"My house was in the middle of the block, kind of making it the natural meeting place. Denny's house was across the street, and come to think of it, his house was in the middle of the block too, only on the upper side. Hmm...being on the upper side must have had something to do with it not being a good place to meet." Granddad

mulled that over for a moment and then continued, "Chuck lived all the way down on the corner of Tenth and Piedmont. His house used to be a grocery store. Can you imagine that? Living in a grocery store!

"Of course, grocery stores were different when I was your age. They were much smaller and there were many more of them. It seemed like every neighborhood had its own, sometimes two or three. They didn't have as many choices in the kinds of foods you could buy like the stores have today, but they had something much better..." Granddad's eyes opened wide, "penny candy counters!

"Candy was on display inside a glass counter, and we could pick and choose what we wanted the storekeeper to put in a little brown paper bag. I'll have one of those...and...umm...one of those...and...umm...one of those..." Granddad pointed with his finger while he pretended to be peering through glass. "There were chocolate cookies, Tootsie Rolls, gummy candy, malted milk balls, all kinds of wonderful things, even baseball cards with bubble gum! The man behind the counter would be patient for a while, but then reminded us that he had other work to do and that he couldn't stand there all day waiting for us to decide.

"I always thought it was a shame they took the candy counter out when they closed the old grocery store Chuck lived in. Think of how fun it would have been for us if it had still been there..." Granddad drifted away for a few seconds, revisiting a cherished memory. "BUT! That's not what this story is about!" His return startled the children into even greater anticipation. He leaned forward once again and spoke in a very quiet voice as though he was going to share a secret. "Our neighborhood was full of adventure," he glanced over the heads of his grandchildren to meet the eyes of his daughter, who was leaning against the kitchen door-jam while wiping her hands on a dish towel, then added in a whisper, "and this one...was our best adventure ever."

Granddad cherished this opportunity of taking his grandchildren into his past. He had told these children many stories, but none had been his own. Tonight they were going to meet his childhood friends.

"Chuck and I were not the most talented kids when we were eleven years old, unless you think building model cars and wooden carts takes talent, but Denny...oh, Denny...how he could draw. Why, he could take one look at a bird sitting on a branch and draw it to perfection. He could draw cars and army tanks and airplanes. I don't think there was anything he couldn't draw.

"Chuck and I couldn't draw at all, but we had imaginations, and our imaginations kept us very busy!

One day we would be cops and robbers, on another - astronauts, and on another - pirates. One of our favorite things to be was cowboys. We had cowboy hats and bandanas, holsters with six-shooters, western shirts and cowboy boots. We also had a cowgirl!

"Sam lived on the upper side of Ninth Street, right across the back alley from my house. Of course, her real name wasn't Sam, it was Samantha. She was what you would call a tomboy. There were girls in the neighborhood she could play with, but she would much rather play with us. The other girls wore dresses, played with dolls, and had tea parties. Nothing wrong with that I suppose, but Sam wasn't having fun unless she was rolling in the dirt, or hitting a baseball, or doing any of the other exciting things us boys would do.

"This was my circle of friends: Chuck, Denny and Sam. The four of us were always on the lookout for adventure. Sometimes we found it, and sometimes it found us." Granddad put on his story telling face and began in earnest...

~~~

GRANDDAD'S STORY

# Chapter 2

"Chucky! Chuuuuucky!" It was already eight o'clock in the morning and Chuck had failed to show up at the meeting place. Jess had been out riding his bike for an hour already. *I wonder what's wrong. Maybe he fell out of bed, broke his arm, and his dad had to rush him to the hospital! Maybe he got food poisoning from something he ate and he can't get out of bed at all!* "Chucky!" Chuck's bedroom was right next to the back door. Jess yelled loud enough for the whole neighborhood to hear. Surely his best friend would hear him if he was able.

The inside door creaked as it slowly opened. Chuck stood behind the wooden screen door rubbing his eyes.

"Are you all right, Chuck? You didn't meet me! I thought for sure something happened to you!"

Chuck was still half asleep. "Nothing happened. I just overslept."

"Overslept! That's all? You just overslept?"

"I'm too tired to come up with a better story. We went to the drive-in theater last night and didn't get home until midnight."

A drive-in theater was a wonderful place to go. Moms and dads would dress their little kids in pajamas and the whole family would sit in the car and watch a movie on a huge outdoor screen. There would always be an intermission in the movie so families could go to the concession stand and load up on popcorn and pop and candy.

"I'll be out in ten minutes."

Jess sat down on the top step of the back porch stairway. This warm muggy summer morning had gotten off to a slow start. He was glad his friend was OK, but disappointed Chuck didn't have a better story to tell. He rested his chin in his hand and thought, *oh well, things are bound to get more exciting when Sam comes out to play.*

The two best friends mounted their bikes and headed to the meeting place where Denny and Sam were patiently waiting. Chuck had a brand new bike with high handle bars and a banana seat, AND it had three speeds! He was very proud of his new bike and wouldn't let anyone else ride it. Jess' bike was old. His dad won it in a poker game. It was too big for Jess, but his dad said he would just have to grow into it. Denny and Sam also had older bikes, but at least they were the right size. All four children were dressed in the outfits agreed upon the day before. This was going to be a cowboy day.

"Everybody got their six-shooters?" Jess took inventory to make sure a pirate's sword hadn't found its way into somebody's holster. Things had to be authentic.

"Yup."

"I've got mine."

"Me too."

"OK. Now remember, our bikes are our horses so we can't just throw them down when we stop. We have to tie them up to a tree so they don't run off."

"My bike, ah…I mean my horse won't run off. I have to peddle it to make it move."

"Come on, Denny, play along." Jess turned to Chuck and said, "We're going to have to get him an imagination for his next birthday."

"I've got an imagination…it's just different than yours."

"Yeah, so different that we have to keep explaining everything to you."

"Where we heading today, Jess?" Sam counted on Jess to lead, but once the plan was made she found lots of ways to add excitement.

"We're going to ride up the El Paso Trail. I heard the outlaws that robbed the bank yesterday were camped in the woods up there. There's a fifty dollar reward on each of their heads. The way I figure it, four outlaws captured means fifty dollars for each of us."

"Fifty dollars! WOW! What I could buy with that!" Chuck immediately started spending the make-believe reward money on all kinds of treasures.

The El Paso Trail headed north up Twenty-fourth Avenue West and then turned west onto Skyline Drive. The south side of Skyline was a drop-off with boulders, bushes, and small trees scattered down the hillside. Way down at the bottom, past the houses and streets and alleys, ran the St. Louis River which in turn ran into the western tip of the second largest freshwater lake in the world, Lake Superior. On pirate days the four friends found themselves behind the stone-walled overlook, defending their fortress against cannon balls lobbed from ships below. On this cowboy day, though, they turned their attention to the north side of the El Paso and tied their horses to birch trees.

"We'll spread out here and meet at the cave to go over any sign we might find. We're looking for boot prints with a broken heel."

"We always meet at the cave. Can't we meet someplace else this time?" Sam wanted to discover new territory.

Denny's face paled, he wanted to meet at the cave

because he knew where it was. He was not good with direction in the woods, and he had no desire to get lost.

Chuck put his arm around Denny's shoulder and said, "We'll meet at the cave so our adventure doesn't turn into a search party."

One hour of hard tracking produced no clues to the whereabouts of the outlaws, at least not amongst the three cowboys who found their way to the cave. Sam was still out in the woods somewhere.

Jess placed his two index fingers under his tongue and let loose with a shrill whistle. Everyone stood still, listening for a response…nothing. "I hope she didn't run into a bear. Make sure your guns are loaded boys. We may need to use 'em."

Chuck spotted Sam before the boys could take one step. "There she is…over there making her way through that alder brush. She's got something in her hands…a box or something."

Sam thrashed her way through the thick brush, emerging with a scratch on her right cheek.

"Why'd you come through there, Sam? You know better than to fight that brush." Jess took a look at the scratch, "Does it hurt?"

"Naw, I've had worse from sliding into first. I didn't want to be followed."

"Followed by who?"

"By whoever left this box."

"What do you got there?" All three boys circled around Sam as she plopped down on a rock and placed the box in her lap.

"A strongbox."

"What's a strongbox?"

"Come on, Denny, every cowboy knows what a strongbox is."

"Well I don't. And I'm not a real cowboy anyway, just a pretend one."

"You tell him, Chuck, I'm tired of having to explain things."

Chuck was patient with Denny. He knew Denny would rather be sitting on his front porch sketching a picture of a squirrel on a tree branch than running through the woods with them. He was only there because he knew his friends had no interest in sitting with him to draw. "A strongbox is where money was kept on a stagecoach. You know, like when we watch the cowboy movies and the stage gets robbed. The robbers are always telling the driver (here Chuck pulls his gun and takes the pose of an outlaw), 'All right mister, throw down the strongbox.'"

Denny got the picture. "You mean we're chasing REAL robbers?"

All four looked at each other as if a light suddenly came on in a dark room. After all, this was a real strongbox, and what would a real strongbox be doing in a make believe adventure?

"Where'd you find it, Sam?" Jess took a good look at the box. It was dirty and a bit scratched up, and it had an old padlock on the latch.

"I tripped over it on the path after we split up. A corner of it was sticking out of the dirt. I've walked that path a hundred times and never tripped over it before. It must have been sticking out farther this time. I wonder how many other people have walked over it, or even stepped on it, and never knew it was there?... Anyway, after I fell, I looked back to see what tripped me. It didn't look like a rock or part of a stump sticking out of the ground so I started to dig around it. That's what took me so long to meet up with you guys, the ground was hard and it took a long time to get it out."

Chuck took the box from Sam's lap and gave it a good shake. Sounds like there's something inside, but it's pretty light, maybe a piece of paper."

"Maybe it's a million dollar bill!" Sam's face lit up with excitement.

Jess lightheartedly informed Sam, "There's no such thing as a million dollar bill."

17

"We could pretend there is until we get the box open."

Sam's excitement caused Chuck to chuckle at Jess' predicament, "Let's see, we can pretend our bikes are horses, and we can pretend that we're cowboys, but we can't pretend there's a million dollar bill?"

Jess ignored the question and fell deep into thought. After a few moments he delightfully exclaimed, "We don't have to pretend!"

Sam jumped right in, "You mean there IS a million dollar bill?"

"No, I mean we don't have to pretend we're cowboys, or pirates, or anything else for adventure. We have a REAL adventure staring us in the face. This is a REAL box, and we don't know where it came from or what's in it. We don't know how long it's been buried, and we don't know who buried it. We've got a mystery on our hands, and we have to solve it!"

"So now we'll pretend we're detectives?"

"We don't have to pretend, Sam. We'll be REAL detectives because we have a REAL mystery that has to be solved."

"So if we open the box and find a blank piece of paper should we pretend it has something on it or do you want me to draw a treasure map for you?" Denny raised his eyebrows a couple of times, letting Jess know he could help their adventure along if he wanted him to.

"Oh, there'll be something on it. Nobody puts a piece of paper in a strongbox, locks it up and buries it, unless there's something of value connected to it. Yes sir, this could be our best adventure ever! Come on, let's head home and break this box open."

GRANDDAD'S STORY

# Chapter 3

The sound of bike tires sliding on a gravel strewn concrete alley was music to the four friend's ears. Their speed always increased before they hit the brakes and threw their bikes sideways. The amount of rocks plastering sides of garages was the measure of success.

Jess' dad's garage was old. Parts of the wooden lap siding were spongy from decades of exposure to rain and snow. The smell of wood rot from the walls mixed with the smell of blackened engine oil and spilled brake fluid that had soaked into the timber floor made you hold your breath when you first stepped through the door. The single overhead seventy-five watt light bulb struggled to provide enough light in this one stall building with no windows. Those who entered on a sunny day had to allow time for their eyes to adjust to keep from tripping over something. Jess never liked entering this dungeon, but he loved the tools it contained.

Jess' dad worked on cars, and he had every tool needed to do any job. Jess was privileged to use these tools because he always put them back exactly where he found them. It's not that Jess was a perfect kid. He only made his bed sometimes, and his idea of a clean bedroom was not the same as his mom's idea of a clean bedroom, but he knew if he wanted to use tools he would have to respect his dad's rules.

Chuck, Sam and Denny huddled close behind Jess as he clamped the strongbox in the vise and began to pry the latch with a large screwdriver. Each detective was desperately trying to be the first to catch a glimpse of whatever the box held.

"Hey, you gotta stop breathing down my neck. I need room to work here." Jess pried at the latch for several minutes before abandoning the screwdriver idea. He reached for his dad's large sledgehammer and metal chisel. Sam ducked as Jess drew his arm back for a mighty blow. The lock remained intact, but the latch broke free from the cover. Eight eyes stared at the box as if it was going to open by itself to reveal its secret. Finally, Jess slowly raised the cover. He was almost afraid to peer inside, fearing their adventure might be over before it began.

"LOOK!" Sam's shout just about blew out Jess' eardrum. "Maybe it IS a treasure map!"

A piece of cloth folded into a three inch square lay on the bottom of the box. Fine dust fell from between the folds as Jess raised it from its hiding place and began to open what they all hoped would be the start to their best adventure ever.

"There's writing on it."

"What does it say?" The question came from three voices in unison.

"I don't know...the writing's faded. Let's go outside in the sunlight and see if we can read it."

Jess put the hammer and chisel back on the tool rack, took the strongbox from the vice, and led the others outside to the picnic table in his back yard. Everyone knelt on the benches so they could lean over to get a close look at the writing.

Chuck tried to make out the words: "'My name is Henry Mattson and I am...' can you make out what's next?"

Denny squinted to try and focus, "'...leaving' I think it says, 'leaving this world'."

"I think you're right, Denny, 'leaving this world.'" Chuck lifted his eyes from the cloth and looked around at his friends, "he must be going to die!"

"I'd say he died a long time ago." Jess gave the strongbox a nudge with his hand, "look how old this thing is. I bet it's a hundred years old or more."

The thought of a hidden treasure was exciting enough,

but to have the added mystery of a treasure that might be over a hundred years old caused the four friends to stare at each other in wonder.

Chuck raised the cloth up and held it in the direct sunlight to try and see the words better. "I think I can read the whole thing, '...leaving this world. I can't take this treasure with me so I will leave it here for you to find. I say 'you' because you are the one reading this note, which means you found my strongbox. If there are two of you, or maybe three or four, don't worry, there's enough treasure for everyone."

The four kids looked at each other with eyes wide and mouths open. "Enough treasure for everyone! How much do you think there is, Jess?"

"I don't know, Sam, but it sounds like we're going to be rich!"

The friends began to jump around, hooting and hollering and slapping each other on the back as if they had done something great. After calming down Jess turned to Chuck and said, "Read the rest of the note, it's gotta say where the treasure is."

Chuck held the cloth note in the sunlight again and continued on, "Walk 105 yards north and 52 yards east and you'll find a cave."

"A cave? Our cave?" Jess looked puzzled. "We've been

in that cave a million times. There's no treasure there."

"Wait, Jess, there's more. 'Walk 25 feet straight ahead into the cave and dig 2 feet into the dirt.' ...There must be another strongbox!"

"We'll need something to dig with if the dirt is as hard as it was where I found this box. Two feet down is a long ways." Sam held her hand out above the ground trying to take measure.

"We might need a dirt pick if the ground is that hard." Jess knew his dad didn't have a dirt pick so he looked around at the others.

"My dad's got one!" Denny was excited to be able to pitch in.

"Great! Go home and get it and I'll grab my dad's shovel out of the garage."

"I won't be able to come back right away."

"Why not?" Jess sounded agitated.

"Cause my mom said I had to be home for lunch at 11:30, and we'll never have time to dig it out and be back by then. I'll have to wait until after lunch."

"Denny! This is REAL TREASURE we're talking about!" Jess was genuinely agitated now.

"I know, but my mom's got a friend coming for lunch, and she said I had to be home and cleaned up by 11:30."

"What if somebody gets to our treasure before we do?

It will be your fault, Denny." Sam was just as impatient as Jess.

"Guys...the treasure has been waiting for us in that cave for a long time. I don't think another couple of hours are going to hurt." Chuck was usually the voice of reason in situations like this. "Besides, we have the note that tells where the treasure is. Nobody else knows about it."

"And let's make sure nobody finds out about it." Jess spoke as if giving an order. "Our lips are sealed, right?... RIGHT?"

"Right." The response was unanimous.

"So you'll wait for me?" Denny had been left out of things before. He didn't want to be left out of the first adventure he was really enjoying, especially when there was treasure involved.

"What else can we do?" Jess grudgingly said, "You've got the pick!"

# Chapter 4

Denny's mom's lunch took longer than expected. It was 2:30 in the afternoon before he joined his friends with the dirt pick, and it was 3:15 before they found themselves in the cave.

"Twenty-five feet, boy that brings us almost to the back of the cave. Do you think this is right?" Chuck stood scratching the back of his head as if that would make him think better.

"That's what the note said." Jess tried to grab the dirt pick from Denny's hand.

Denny resisted, "I'll take the first few whacks."

"Be my guest."

Denny swung the pick hard and struck the ground. The pick handle vibrated right out of his hands from the force of the blow. "Ouch! That stung! Feels like rock, not dirt."

Jess dropped to his knees and brushed a top layer of dirt away. "It is rock. This can't be right."

"But it's twenty-five feet straight in from the entrance to the cave just like the note says." Chuck scratched the back of his head again.

Jess began brushing dirt away all around the spot, "Rock! Nothing but rock!" He crawled further from the measured area, "This whole floor is rock."

"How can that be? He couldn't have buried the treasure in rock." Sam fell to her knees and checked for herself.

Chuck, still scratching his head and still thinking, said, "What if this isn't the right cave?"

Everyone stopped and stared at Chuck.

"There is no other cave." Jess voiced what the others were thinking.

"How do you know?"

"Because we've never seen another cave, and we've been all through these woods."

"Just because we haven't seen it doesn't mean it doesn't exist. We've never looked for another cave. Maybe it's not easy to see. Maybe you have to stumble over it like Sam stumbled over the strongbox. And besides, we never measured out the distance like the man in the note told us to do. We just figured he was talking about our cave."

"Chuck's got a point there, Jess." Sometimes Denny was happy to take sides against Jess.

"Well, let's go pace it off then. I bet it leads us right back here." Jess didn't like to be challenged.

"I think we're going to have to do better than pace it off, I think we have to measure it."

"Um...I think so too." Sam never liked to go against Jess, but sometimes Chuck made more sense.

"OK...OK, but that means we have to go home to get something to measure with and you know we won't be able to come back here today. It'll be too close to supper when we get home, and our folks won't let us come up here at night."

"We'll just have to come tomorrow morning then. We can meet after supper and decide what we're going to use to measure with and figure out if we need anything else, like flashlights maybe. The entrance to the new cave might be really small. Maybe that's why we've never seen it. And then...after we've made our plans...we can dream about how we're going to spend all of our money!" Chuck had already begun to dream. He was going to buy all the model cars on the shelves at the hobby shop, and then get a new fishing pole, and new hockey skates, and on and on his dreams went.

"The first thing I'm going to get is a new bike." Jess stood up and brushed the dirt off his knees. "And my bike is going to have TEN speeds." He gave Chuck a look while thinking; *mine's going to be better than yours.*

"Me too, and it will be a boys bike, not a sissy girls

bike!" Sam didn't like the fact that her old bike was pink and the center bar was lowered to make it easier for girls to mount.

Chuck put his arm around Denny's shoulder, "How about you, Den, you got any plans?"

"Paper...and pencils...colored pencils, every color they make, and lots of picture frames so I can hang my pictures on the wall in my bedroom."

"What? No new bike?" Jess couldn't understand not wanting a new bike.

"I won't need a bike if I have enough paper and pencils to draw all day."

"Man, you're weird." Jess was convinced Denny knew nothing about how to have fun.

The four dreamers left the shovel and pick in the cave and walked down the gentle wooded slope to where they had left their bikes. When they arrived they were met by an unwelcome discovery.

"My bike...where's my bike?" At first Chuck was composed as he walked in both directions kicking the tall grass away with his feet. Soon, though, he became frantic, "It's gone! Gone! SOMEBODY STOLE MY BIKE!"

Jess could see how angry his friend was becoming. Chuck's face turned red and his fists were clenched. In a way Jess felt sorry for him, and in a way he didn't. *Serves you right. You've been selfish about your bike ever since you got it. You never let me, or Sam, or Denny try it even once.* Jess felt bad about what he was thinking, but only for a moment.

"I worked hard for that bike! I cut lawns and shoveled snow, and saved my birthday money just to be able to buy it! Who would take it?... If I ever find out I'm going to fix him good! He'll be sorry! He won't even be able to ride a bike because I'm going to break both his legs!"

Jess, Sam and Denny had never seen Chuck so angry. No one was willing to breathe a word for fear of saying the wrong thing. Chuck kicked at the ground, spraying dirt against the other bikes. He turned and headed toward home.

Chuck decided not to show up at the meeting place after supper. He was so angry he didn't want to be around his friends. *I'll have to walk everywhere now and those guys will get to ride their bikes. It's not fair, it's just not fair. I had the nicest bike...and now I've got nothing.*

The other three detectives met at the appointed time and the appointed place, the picnic table in Jess' back yard. They drew up a list of stuff they would need for the next morning's adventure: a twenty-five foot tape measure, flashlights, water, and a sandwich apiece. The search for the cave could take a while, and the dig might take even longer. No one wanted to head back home for lunch in the middle of this adventure.

"Do you think Chuck will come with us in the morning?" Denny sometimes believed Chuck was his only real friend. He felt like he was in the way on most adventures and always thought Jess really didn't want him there. As for Sam, Denny didn't think she cared one way or the other. But Chuck looked out for him, and he was glad for that.

"Oh, he'll be here. He's going to want to find the treasure more than ever now. He needs a new bike."

Sam looked across the picnic table and asked, "Jess...do you think that maybe we should all leave our bikes at home and walk tomorrow so Chuck doesn't feel bad?"

"Are you kidding? We'll be walking part of the way up anyway because we have to push our bikes up Twenty-forth. The rest of the way we'll try to ride double."

"But your bike is the only one that's big enough to ride double. Do you want to do that?"

"Got no choice. We can't look for the treasure without all four of us being there. "

**"JESS!"**

"That's my dad, I gotta go. Meet you guys up front in the morning at the regular time. I'll get the tape measure from my dad's tools. See ya." Jess jumped up from the picnic table and headed for the garage. "You want me, dad?"

"What I want is my shovel. You seen it?"

"Ah...yeah, I ah...borrowed it this morning."

"Well, where is it?"

Jess knew he had blown it. He looked down at the garage floor and confessed. "It's in our cave...above the boulevard."

"It's where?"

"In our cave... You see, we found this treasure. Well, we haven't found it yet, but we will, and we have to dig for it..."

"You're not making much sense, son. Just tell me why my shovel isn't where it's supposed to be."

"I didn't think you would need it tonight, and I didn't want to carry it home and then carry it right back up again in the morning."

"What's the rule?"

"Put it back where it belongs when you're done with it... But, Dad, I wasn't done with it."

"Well, you're done with it now. The first thing I want you to do in the morning is go up there and bring that shovel home. You put it right here so I know where to find it tomorrow night... Understand?"

"Yes." Jess asked a question he already knew the answer to. "I suppose this means I can't borrow your tape measure for tomorrow?"

Jess' dad just gave him a look. "I'm going next door to see if I can borrow John's shovel. You head in the house and help your mom with the supper dishes."

# Chapter 5

Jess was on his bike by 7 a.m., heading to the cave to retrieve the shovel. He would have to break the news to the rest of the gang that he not only didn't have a tape measure for their search, but he also no longer had a shovel for their dig. The other kids' dads had already left for work so they couldn't ask permission for the tools they needed. They would just have to come up with some other solutions.

Jess tied the shovel to his handle bars and started peddling. When he turned off Skyline Drive and began his coast down the hill, his back wheel started to shake. He pushed back on the pedal with his foot to hit the brake, but before he knew it he and his bike were flying through the air. He landed with a thud on the grassy hill next to the sidewalk.

Jess grimaced as he pushed the bike off his right leg. His jeans were torn and blood oozed from the gash on the inside of his calf. He maneuvered himself into a sitting position and tried to get a better look at his injury.

"Are you all right?" The question came from a man

who had stopped his pick-up truck and leaned over to roll down the passenger side window.

"I don't know… It's bleeding pretty bad." Jess worked hard to hold back tears.

The man pulled his truck to the side of the avenue and got out to check on the accident victim. "Why…you're Jess."

"Mr. Crowley!"

"You've grown some since you were in my first grade class. That was a pretty short flight you took there. Bikes don't fly too far without wings, you know."

"Yeah, I found that out."

Mr. Crowley kneeled down and probed the area of Jess' injury, "Your leg looks like it'll be OK, just a nasty cut. Let's get you home so your mom can work her magic."

Jess stood and limped to the truck while Mr. Crowley loaded the broken bike. The first grade teacher shut the driver's door, shifted into gear and continued the conversation, "Interesting way to carry a shovel. You out digging for gold this morning?"

Jess' eyes got big, "How did you know? I mean…" Jess closed his mouth to give himself time to think. "I left the shovel in our cave yesterday, and I had to go get it for my dad this morning." He said nothing else, hoping Mr.

Crowley wouldn't ask anymore questions.

Mr. Crowley had a half smile on his face as he looked straight ahead, paying attention to his driving. He was wise enough to let summer tales of young boys remain amongst friends.

Mr. Crowley stopped in front of Jess' dad's garage to drop off the injured passenger and his bike. "Here's what caused your accident, Jess," he pointed to the rear wheel mounting slots. "The steel is rusted...looks like it finally gave way. It's a good thing it broke loose at the top of the hill and not farther down when your speed would have been much greater."

"Rusted? Why would it be rusted?"

"Well, let's see, have you ever ridden your bike in the rain, or splashed through puddles, or left it out overnight so that it was drenched with dew in the morning?"

Jess knew he had done all those things.

"That's how things rust. Water will eventually win out over steel."

"Do you think it can be fixed?"

"I don't know...looks pretty rusty to me. Steel can be welded, but not when rust has eaten away at it. This has rusted from the inside out, which means water has gotten inside the pipe. It looks way too thin to weld. You're probably going to have to look for another bike."

This was not good news to Jess. His parents were not rich, and they were not going to go out and buy him another bike. Now he and Chuck were both going to have to depend on the treasure if they were ever going to ride again.

"Hey, Jess, what are doing back here? I thought we were going to meet up front?" Sam was pushing her bike across the alley when she began talking. She noticed Jess' torn pant leg and the now dried blood that was on it. "What happened to you?"

"I flipped my bike."

"Are you hurt bad?"

"No, but I've got to go in and have my mom take a look at it. I might be a while. I'm sure she'll want to clean it out." This was not Jess' first experience with deep cuts. "Better tell the guys that I'll be out as soon as I can."

"We'll wait for you." Just then Sam saw the bike. "Oh no!"

Mr. Crowley gave a chuckle and said, "I'll leave you kids to your problems. Hope you have a better rest of the day, Jess."

"Thank you for helping me, Mr. Crowley."

Mr. Crowley gave a wave of his hand, jumped in his truck and was off.

"Jess, your bike is broken!"

"No kidding."

"You won't be riding double on that today."

"I won't be riding double OR single on that bike ever again. It's junk." Jess stared at his bike and shook his head. "I know it was old and too big for me, but I loved riding that bike. Shoot, I just love riding. It's going to be one boring rest of the summer if we don't find that treasure."

Sam brought her bike back home and put it away while Jess went in the house to be attended to. By 8:30 a.m. the four were together at the meeting place. Jess filled his friends in on his accident and then explained why they no longer had a tape measure and shovel available to them.

"What are we going to do? We have to have something to measure with." Sam was addressing her question to Jess, as she usually did, but it was Denny who spoke up.

"I've got a really long rope!"

"What good will that do if we don't know how long it is?" Jess couldn't grasp the potential Denny saw in his rope.

"We measure it against something we do know the length of."

Chuck piped in, "That's a great idea, Denny." He struck his thinking pose until he let loose with, "I've got it! We know how long our fort is because we used eight foot boards on the floor."

"Sure, that'll do it." Jess said this as if he believed the rope was a good idea from the start. "We'll go to the fort first and then go and start measuring from where Sam found the strongbox. Has everyone got their flashlight and sandwich?" Jess once again considered himself in charge and was pleased when all nodded their heads yes.

"What about a shovel?"

"Hey, you're on the ball this morning, Denny. Way to go!" Sam gave Denny a smile and a slap on the back, "We would have looked pretty dumb getting up there and have nothing to dig with. My brother has a small fold-up camping shovel. I bet he'll let us use that."

"I just thought about something else too."

"What?" Jess sounded a little short with Denny, almost like he was coming up with too many important details.

"We gotta know which way north is... We need a compass."

Everyone looked at each other. How could they have overlooked their need for a compass? The subject never came up in their planning meeting even though they knew they had to measure in certain directions.

"What would we do without you this morning, Den?

I'll ask my brother if we can borrow his shovel AND compass. I'll be right back. I gotta catch him before he leaves for work." Sam took off running.

Chuck turned to Denny and said, "You better put your bike away unless you want to be the only one riding."

As Denny turned and headed home with his bike, Jess asked Chuck, "Are you still mad...about your bike I mean?"

"Sure I'm still mad, and if I ever find out who took it I'll show him just how mad I am. But...I got to thinking last night that when we find the treasure today I can just go buy a brand new one."

"But yours was brand new."

"Brand new? My bike was two months old already."

"Two months old is new to me. Look how old my bike was."

"Don't you see, Jess, we're going to be rich! After today we can buy a new bike every week if we want."

"Do you think there'll be that much treasure?"

"There's gotta be. Don't you remember what the note said? 'There's enough treasure for everyone.' I'm telling you, we're going to be rich!"

"Yeah...yeah, we are...and then we can get anything we want. I think I'm going to like being rich!"

## GRANDDAD'S STORY

# Chapter 6

The walk up the hill took a toll on Jess' injury. He was having a hard time keeping up with the others. "Could you guys slow down a little, my leg is really hurting."

"We're already going slow." Chuck seemed to be the most driven.

"Well not slow enough. I'm starting to bleed again."

"Maybe we should stop and let him rest." Sam addressed her concern to Chuck.

"OK, we'll let him rest, but I want to make sure we find that treasure today. I need a new bike!"

The four sat down on the grass at the top of Twenty-forth Avenue West for a five minute break, fifteen minutes later they were at the spot where Sam had found the strongbox.

"So, the rope is thirty feet long and we have to go 157 yards," Chuck was scratching the back of his head again. "If the rope is thirty feet that means it's ten yards, and if we have to go 157 yards...hmmm...?" The others waited for Chuck to come up with the answer because he was better at math than the rest of them. "We have to stretch the rope out fifteen times plus another seven yards, or twenty-one feet. That would be just over two-thirds of the length of the rope. You point the direction, Sam, you've got the compass."

"But didn't the note say 105 yards north and fifty-two yards east? We've gotta know how many times to stretch the rope before we turn east."

"You're right again, Denny. Sure glad we got you with us this morning." Chuck took his thinking pose once again. "Let's see, our rope is ten yards long and ten goes into 105...umm...ten and one-half times, then we turn east and go another five times, pace off the last two yards, and we should be at the caves front door!"

Denny was now satisfied. He took one end of the rope and stood on the spot where the strongbox was found. Chuck took the other end of the rope and followed Sam as she began to walk through the woods. Jess picked up the small shovel and waited for Denny to walk up to where Chuck stopped. This was repeated through woods that were sometimes sparse and sometimes thick. Chuck turned east once they reached their northern most destination and followed Sam again. Their measurements brought them to the back side of a very familiar hill.

"There must be a back entrance to our cave." Jess was certain their cave was the only cave in the woods, and he was tired of being wrong.

"It can't go into our cave, Jess. Our cave is one room with no way in or out except the one we know about. Besides, this is a big hill. There could be another cave here somewhere." Chuck dropped his end of the rope and began to push brush away. After several minutes of searching he discovered a pile of rocks behind thick fern growth. "Look at this, guys!"

"What is it?" Jess ran, favoring his sore leg, over to where Chuck was standing.

"These rocks could be covering the entrance!"

"Well, don't just stand there, let's find out!" Sam squeezed her way between Chuck and Jess and began to throw rocks to the side before the boys even had a chance to bend over. Denny stood back, believing there would be no room for a fourth. When the rocks where cleared the three stood and stared.

"Nothing!" Chuck's face was red and full of sweat. "Nothing but dirt!" He kicked at the side of the hill and then stomped the dirt where the rocks had stood. In an instant he was on the ground.

"His leg...IT'S DISAPPEARED!" Denny Stood pointing at the hole Chuck's leg had fallen through while Jess and Sam grabbed Chuck's shirt and pulled him back.

"That was close! I could have fallen right in!"

"I don't think you would have fit through that hole." Jess knelt down and attempted to peer through the darkness. "Can't see a thing." He took his flashlight from his pocket, lay on the ground and squeezed his arm and head through the opening.

"See anything now?" Chuck rubbed his leg as he asked the question.

Jess struggled back out and sat up. "It's a cave, that's for sure. It looks like it goes right under our cave… You know what that means?" Everyone looked at Jess for the answer. "The rock floor in our cave is really the ceiling in this cave."

"Hey," Denny seemed amused by the insight, "we've been walking on top of another cave and never knew it. You guys thought you knew everything about these woods, always telling me I couldn't get lost. What if you find another hole and fall into it and nobody sees you go through because you're alone. I wasn't scared all this time…I was smart!"

"You might be right, Denny, there could be other holes out here that don't have rocks over them. Maybe we better travel in pairs from now on." Chuck was still rubbing his leg.

"Can we get down there, Jess?" Sam had visually sized up the hole, thinking it too small to squeeze a body through.

"Not unless we make the hole bigger. Why don't you and Denny go to our cave and get the pick, maybe we can whack away at it until one of us can fit through the hole."

Sam didn't like the sound of that. She was the smallest. Enjoying an adventure with her friends was one thing, being dropped into a black hole that no one had been down in years was quite another.

Jess and Chuck discussed a plan while Sam and Denny went for the pick.

"How far down to the bottom?" Chuck was the biggest so he figured he would not get a chance to go through the hole himself.

"It looked like it might be about ten to twelve feet."

"Whoever goes down there has to do the digging."

"Yeah, I know. Maybe Sam and I can both get through the hole and then we can switch off. I don't think Denny is going to want to go down there."

"Probably not... We can tie the rope to that tree for you to slide down."

"I wonder if there are any animals in there?"

"Only if there's another way in."

"Bats don't need a very big hole to go in and out of... I hate bats."

**"DUCK! THERE"S ONE NOW!"**

Jess swung his arms up over his head and hit the ground. Chuck laughed so hard he could barely speak, "I...I got you good... You should have seen your face."

"Thanks a lot. Now all I'm going to think about when I'm in that cave is BATS!"

"Oh, but it was funny...really funny..." Chuck was still forcing words out between laughs.

Jess saw no humor in his heart almost stopping, "Come on. Let's get the rope tied around that tree."

Denny took only three swings with the pick to loosen some dirt. The ground was not as hard as Jess thought it would be. The hole was large enough to drop through in no time at all.

"I'll go down first, Sam. Are you OK with this?"

"I guess so. It is an adventure...right?" Sam's voice quivered.

"The best one we've ever had, and when we come up...we'll be rich!"

Sam shined her flashlight down the hole as Jess began to slide down the rope. When Jess hit the floor he took his flashlight out of his pocket and turned it on. He had come down next to the wall. The cave was larger than the one above. It was damp and dark. He shined his light across the ceiling. No bats.

"I'm coming down, Jess. Shine your light on the rope."

Sam hit the floor of the cave with a thud, having let go of the rope and dropping the last three feet.

"You all right, Sam?" Jess reached down to give her his hand.

"I'm OK. I thought I was closer to the bottom than that. The ground sure is wet." Sam tried to brush the wetness from her pants.

"We better check to see if there are any holes down here. I don't want to fall down another level."

Two light beams scanned the floor. Jess began to inch forward, testing the ground before he put his full weight into his step. Sam was on Jess' heels with her hand clamped to his shirt, ready to pull him back from any pitfall he might encounter.

"Are you guys all right down there?" Chuck moved his flashlight around in an attempt to locate his two friends.

"We're fine, just checking out the floor. Lower the pick and shovel on the rope."

Denny could hear the echo of Jess' voice. He grabbed both digging tools and laid them next to Chuck. Chuck pulled up the rope and tightly tied the instruments before lowering them into the hole.

Jess was finally satisfied that the floor in the cave was solid. He and Sam had been over the entire area. The cave was another one room chamber, just like the cave above, only larger, with no apparent way in or out other than the hole they entered through.

"We need to measure out twenty-five feet. How are we going to do that? We can't drop the rope down because we need it tied to that tree so we can climb out of here." Sam envisioned Chuck up on the surface scratching the back of his head to come up with a solution.

"I can lie on the ground and reach down the hole, holding one end of the rope. It's thirty feet long so if you butt it to the wall and stretch it out we should only be a few feet short. You can guess that distance."

"What if you drop it? That's our only way out of here." Jess didn't feel all that comfortable with Chuck's plan.

"I won't drop it. What do think I am, a butterfingers?"

Jess and Sam looked at each other and then in unison said, "OK."

Denny untied the rope from the tree and handed it to Chuck. "Maybe you should tie it around your wrist…just in case, I mean."

"Boy, nobody trusts me around here."

Chuck dropped the remaining portion of the rope down the hole while hanging on tight to the loose end. He lay on his stomach and stretched his arm down as far as he could. Sam bent the rope into where the wall met the floor, securing it with her foot to hold the rope in place.

Jess grabbed the other end and walked straight out from where they had entered the cave. He drew a line when he came to a stop and paced off another three feet, making an X to mark the spot.

**"OUCH!"**

Startled, Jess and Sam quickly turned toward the sound of Chuck's voice just in time to see his end of the rope drop to the cave floor. A sick feeling invaded their stomachs. For the first time in his life Jess was sorry he had an imagination. The terror of dark cold nights sleeping on the wet cave floor raced through his mind.

"Something bit me!" Chuck jumped to his feet. The dropped rope wasn't on his mind. Finding the critter that caused the pain was his priority. He pulled his shirt off, shaking it to see if anything would fall out. A bumblebee hit the ground, spinning on its back as its wings flapped in an effort to right itself. Chuck stomped on the bee, exclaiming, "I'll teach you to sting me!"

Denny looked up at Chuck and then down again at the squashed bee. He knew the bee would die anyway, but he didn't like the way Chuck smashed the poor thing into the ground. Denny had once studied a bee that had landed on his knee. The intricate detail of its structure had astounded him. His favorite sketch was of that bee, and now there was another in front of him, ground into the dirt, with every intricate detail indistinguishable.

Chuck noticed the look on Denny's face and began to let go of his anger. "I'm sorry, Denny. I didn't have to do that. I bet you would have liked to study him."

Denny's eyes were still glued to the ugly mess the bee had now become. "It's just a bee... We better see if we can get the rope back up." He turned to face the hole, his mind now more on the bee than the treasure.

Jess cupped his hands and yelled with his head tilted upward, "You guys alive up there?"

"Yeah, we're alive. I got stung. Sorry about dropping the rope." Chuck looked at Denny once more to make sure he really was OK, then turned his attention to the hole and started scratching the back of his head. "What if you tie the rope real tight to the end of the pick handle and raise it up to the hole? I'll reach down as far as I can and try to grab hold of it." Chuck scuffed the ground with his shoe in search of any other critters before lying down.

"That's as high as I can raise it. Can you reach it?"

Chuck's arm and shoulder were as deep into the whole as they could go. He stretched out his fingers until the tips just managed to brush the top of the pick. Jess saw how close Chuck was to grabbing hold so he rose up onto his tiptoes high enough for Chuck to get a grasp.

"I've got it!"

Chuck pulled the pick and the rope through the hole and handed Denny the free end. Denny retied the rope around the tree while Chuck lowered the tool back down to the two anxious treasure hunters.

Jess and Sam laid their flashlights on the cave floor, pointing in the direction of the X scratched in the dirt. The dig began. Jess swung the pick with as much force as he could muster while Sam shoveled away the loose dirt during every break Jess took. Twenty-five minutes of digging produced a three foot deep empty hole.

"We should have hit something by now." Jess wiped sweat from his forehead.

"Maybe we need to dig a little to the right or to the left."

"Maybe. Which way should we go first, Sam? You decide."

"Let's go to the right."

Jess made five swings with the pick. He hit something hard. "That didn't feel like a rock."

Sam fell to her knees and began to drag dirt away with the shovel. Within seconds the corner of a metal box came into view.

"We found it! WE FOUND IT!" Jess yelled in the direction of the cave entrance.

Chuck shined his flashlight in the hole, but the site of

the dig was too far to the side for him to view. "How big is the box? Can we fit it through the hole?" Chuck was sure the treasure was so big that they would have to leave the box in the cave and hand the treasure out piece by piece.

"We haven't got it out yet. Give us some time to dig around it."

"We're rich, Denny! WE'RE RICH!!" Chuck stood up and gave Denny a slap on the back.

"Chuck!"

"I'm here. You got it out?" Chuck had his head sticking in the hole again.

"It's out...and it's the same size as the other box...and just as light."

"What? Another note?"

"I don't know, but it's not gold or silver or anything like that. I'm going to tie it to the rope so you can pull it up and then get us out of here."

When the box was out, Jess and Sam shimmied up the rope like they did in gym class at school. Once again the four kids were gathered around a strongbox with a padlock guarding its secret.

"I'm sure we can break it open with the pick." Chuck didn't wait for an answer. He took hold of the box, placed it on the ground and began swinging at it with the pointed end of the dirt pick. Three hefty blows to the lock broke it open.

The box contained another folded piece of cloth. Dust fell as each fold was opened. There was another message on the cloth...along with something else...holes...lots and lots of holes. Denny reached into the box and picked up the remains of a huge moth while Sam, Chuck and Jess looked at each other in disbelief. There was too little of the message left to even begin to read what had been written.

~~~

# GRANDDAD'S STORY

# Chapter 7

Granddad sat back in his chair, raised his arms and folded his hands behind his head. He gazed upward with a far away look as if there was nothing more to tell.

After a few seconds of silence, Josiah rose to his knees, "Granddad! What happened? You can't stop now! Did they find the treasure?"

Granddad lowered his head and took the time to look at each one of his grandchildren. When he was sure he had their attention he said, "No...and yes."

"I don't get it," Kadin's face twisted with confusion, "how can they not find it, but still find it?"

Em wanted to get something straight, "Is this story really about you and your friends, Granddad, or are you making this up?"

Granddad dropped his hands in his lap and answered, "It really is a story about me and my friends."

"So then you know how it ends."

"Of course I know how it ends."

All the grandchildren were looking at Granddad with

pleading eyes, "Tell us! Please!"

Granddad leaned forward once again, resting his elbows on the arms of the chair and folding his hands in front of him, "Sure I'm going to tell you. You didn't think I would quit there, did you? The best is yet to come."

~~~

"What do we do now, Jess?" Sam was frantic. "How will we find the treasure now?"

"I don't know."

"We won't!" Chuck was mad. He kicked the ground and sent dirt flying. "There's a treasure out here somewhere, and we don't know where to look all because of a big old hungry moth!"

Jess studied the cloth, "Maybe we can guess what the missing letters are and try to make out the message."

"Fat chance... That moth just about ate up the whole alphabet."

Jess knew Chuck was right. He crumpled up the cloth and threw it back in the strongbox. "There goes my new bike. Now I'll be walking all summer...and maybe forever!"

"Well, I HAD a new bike and now I've got nothing!" Chuck abruptly turned from the others and started to walk, "I'm going home. There's no reason to hang around here."

"Wait for me!" Denny grabbed his pick and rope and took off after Chuck while Sam and Jess lagged behind.

"Do you really think there's no hope, Jess? I mean, is there no other way we can find the treasure?"

"I sure don't know how. The only clue we have to keep us searching is that message in the strongbox. Without being able to read it we don't know where to look next. Boy, I had so many things I wanted to buy. The new bike was just going to be the first thing I'd get. I was going to get models and skates and...ah, what does it matter."

"I know what you mean. I've got to keep riding that girl bike now."

"At least you can still ride...but you'll be riding alone."

They made no plans to meet the next day. The loss of the treasure made the thought of any other adventure seem boring. There was still a month left of summer vacation before school would begin. All four children knew the days ahead could not possibly hold as much excitement as the days of their best adventure ever.

The second week of August provided some diversion for the four friends. Each mom had grown tired of the sullen attitudes of their young adventurers. At a mid-afternoon coffee party the moms decided to sign their children up for Bible Club. None of the four children had been to Bible Club in the past so they had no idea what to expect when they arrived for the first meeting that next Monday afternoon.

The club was held in Miss Mabel's yard. Miss Mabel was an elderly lady who had never married. She was short and thin with the most pleasant of smiles. Having no children of her own she loved to treat all the children of the neighborhood like grandchildren. One day a week, all summer long, she made the best chocolate chip cookies and placed them on a plate on her front porch for youngsters to eat.

"Welcome children. I'm so glad you decided to join us for Bible Club this summer. Your mom's have told me of your great disappointment so I hope I can introduce you to a joy that will pick those sad hearts right up. Come around to the backyard, the other kids should be here any minute." A large hand-painted sign proclaimed the theme for the week: TREASURE HUNT!

Miss Mabel noticed faces of gloom staring at the sign. "Is there something wrong children? You all look like you just lost your best friend."

Sam spoke up, "No, nothing's wrong, Miss Mabel. I don't know that we'll be too excited about hunting for treasure, though."

"Well now, how do you know when you don't know

what the treasure is?"

Chuck thought that was a good point, but he also thought that no treasure Miss Mabel had hidden could possibly come close to the treasure of their best adventure ever.

The other children had now arrived. Miss Mabel passed out Bibles to each child. "As you can see on the sign, we are going to be searching for treasure this week." She held up her Bible and said, "This is our treasure map. Is there anyone among you who knows how to read this treasure map?"

If anyone did, no one dared raise their hand.

"You are probably wondering what kind of treasure we could find in a book, especially this book. Well, let me tell you," Miss Mabel's eyes brightened with her smile, "it is lasting treasure.

"I'm going to ask you to open your treasure maps to Matthew 13, verse 44. Some of you may not know how to do that so I'm going to help you." Miss Mabel held her Bible up for all to see. She explained that there were sixty-six different books in the Bible and that each one had its name printed at the top of the page. She then explained that each book had chapters that were numbered and that each chapter had verses that were numbered. She asked the children to search the index for the page number of the book of Matthew, then asked them to find chapter 13, verse 44.

"I'll read verses 44-46 and you follow along as I do. 'The kingdom of heaven is like a treasure hidden in the field, which a man found and hid; and from joy over it he goes and sells all that he has and buys the field. Again, the kingdom of heaven is like a merchant seeking fine pearls, and upon finding one pearl of great value, he went and sold all that he had, and bought it.'

"Have any of you ever found a treasure so valuable that you would give up everything you have for it?" Miss Mabel's high-pitched voice rose even higher with excitement toward the end of her question. "That would have to be a very valuable treasure indeed.

"So...the question is; what makes the treasure of the kingdom of heaven so valuable?" Miss Mabel set her Bible down, turned, and walked into her house. The children looked at each other wondering if that's all there was to the first day of Bible Club. In less than a minute, though, Miss Mabel returned carrying a tray filled to capacity. "I don't expect we'll get too far in our venture without the proper nourishment. I think cake and lemonade will be just the right treats to begin a treasure hunt. Don't you?"

The children yelled their approval and eagerly awaited

their turn at helping to empty the tray.

Fifteen minutes passed before Miss Mabel took the last sip of her lemonade. When she did, she placed her glass on the now empty tray and picked up her Bible. "Let's see if we can find some clues to help us understand what the treasure of the kingdom of heaven is. There was a man who walked on the earth over two thousand years ago. This man's name was Jesus. He told people many parables. Does anyone know what a parable is?"

"I do!" Sam raised her hand as she spoke out. "It's a story."

"That's right. But it's a special kind of story. Do you know what makes it special?"

Sam couldn't answer that question.

"It's special because a parable is meant to teach a moral lesson. By moral I mean something good, something right. Well, this man told some parables about the kingdom of heaven, and they will serve us well as clues. Let's look at one of them and see what we can find out.

"This clue is found in Matthew 13: 31-32. I'll give you all time to find it and then I'll read it to you." When Miss Mabel was satisfied that all were on the correct page, she read, "He presented another parable to them saying, 'The kingdom of heaven is like a mustard seed, which a man took and sowed in his field; and this is smaller than all other seeds; but when it is full grown, it is larger than the garden plants, and becomes a tree, so that the birds of the air come and nest in its branches.' So, does this clue tell us anything about the kingdom of heaven?"

Benny was a boy in the neighborhood who did not come out to play much. He was born with a withered leg. He used crutches to walk and was teased by others, Jess and Chuck amongst them. "It's something that grows?"

"Yes, Benny, it grows! But I'll tell you something extraordinary about the kingdom of heaven, it is already full grown, but when we first come upon it this vast kingdom seems as small as a mustard seed. And a mustard seed is so small that you might not even notice it."

"Then how do you know it's there?" This question came from Peg, one of the girls Sam didn't like playing with because she thought her to be a sissy. Peg was always in a dress and her hair was always in curls. Sam couldn't understand how someone could be so worried about getting dirty.

"Most of the time you don't know that it's there…until it gets big enough for you to take notice."

The children stared with blank faces, not understanding a thing Miss Mabel was saying.

"Let's look at another clue, one right after the one we just read. Verse 33, 'He spoke another parable to them, "The kingdom of heaven is like leaven, which a woman took, and hid in three pecks of meal, until it was all leavened."' What do you think the woman was making?"

"I know that!" Denny was excited to finally be able to give an answer. "Bread!"

"Yes, bread. Have you ever watched your mom make bread? She mixes yeast into the dough (for leaven is like yeast, you know), kneads the dough, covers it with a cloth and lets it sit. You don't know the yeast is there until it begins to work. And what happens when yeast begins to work?"

Peg beat Sam to the punch with this answer, and Sam was not happy about it. "The dough rises!"

"That's right, Peg. So, what can you tell me about the kingdom of heaven from this clue?"

Sam's hand shot up in the air, but when Miss Mabel called on her she paused, as though the answer she was going to give had fallen prey to a deeper thought. She ventured forward slowly, "It...it causes something to change...from the inside out...

"Very good, Samantha, that's a thought we will explore further sometime this week." The group talked more about these clues until Miss Mabel stopped the conversation, "Well, that's enough clues for today. We'll dig into our treasure map again tomorrow and see what else we can find."

"Miss Mabel," Chuck was scratching the back of his head, "you forgot something."

"What did I forget, Chuck?"

"You've told us something about the treasure, but not how to find it." Chuck was secretly hoping that, somehow, finding this treasure would result in a new bike.

"I'm sure you will want to know more about what the treasure is before you decide whether or not you want to find it. Won't you?"

Chuck thought about that. *She's right. If it can't help me get a new bike, why waste my time.*

The four friends huddled on the school playground after Bible Club ended to talk about their afternoon.

"Did you like it, Jess, Bible Club I mean?" Sam was hoping he did.

"It was all right. I don't think I would go back if my mom wasn't making me." Everyone sat silent for a while until Jess spoke again. "What do you think about 'ol gimpy' being there? Haven't seen him out in a while."

"Yeah, I bet we won't play any games all week because gimpy won't be able to do it." Chuck's interest in Bible

Club seemed to be fading fast.

Sam thought she would take her shot, "What about Peg? She won't play any games because her dress might get dirty, or she might mess up her curls."

Chuck turned to the last of the four, "What did you think, Den?"

"I liked it," then he sheepishly added, "I don't mind Benny. It's not his fault he's got a bad leg... He can draw pretty good you know."

"Well, that's something I guess, but who wants to sit around and draw. I'd rather play baseball any day." Jess' remark hurt Denny, but he didn't seem at all sorry for saying it.

"See you guys tomorrow, I gotta help my mom with supper." Sam took off like a sprinter.

## GRANDDAD'S STORY

# Chapter 8

Tuesday brought rain, which meant Bible Club would meet indoors. The friends were curious about what Miss Mabel had up her sleeve for this meeting. "At least we know there'll be something to eat!" Jess was looking for a reason to be happy about spending an hour in Miss Mabel's living room.

"Hello children. Are you ready to go hunting again today?" The children filed in through Miss Mabel's front door, each being handed their treasure map, and were directed to sit anywhere they could find. Peg gracefully took a seat on a Victorian style chair, all the while fluffing her beautiful dress and flowing curls. Sam's mind was screaming, *she thinks she's so beautiful, like a queen. Well she's the ugliest queen I've ever seen.* Sam looked down at her blue jeans and wished she had changed clothes before coming to Bible Club. Jess and Chuck found a patch on the floor, as far away from Benny as possible. Denny seemed hesitant, almost like he was going to sit next to Benny on the couch, but settled for the floor halfway between the couch and his friends. Sam filled in the floor space between Denny and Jess, hoping her dirty jeans wouldn't leave soil on Miss Mabel's carpet.

"Yesterday we learned that the kingdom of heaven holds great value. We then discovered that, even though the kingdom of heaven is full grown, it seems as small as a mustard seed when we first come upon it. We also learned that we probably won't know we have found the kingdom of heaven until it grows big enough for us to take notice. Finally, Samantha stumbled on a wonderful thought, that the kingdom of heaven causes change...from the inside out.

"Let's open our treasure maps to Mark 4: 26-29." Miss Mabel paused until all eyes were looking in her direction. "I want to first mention that our treasure map sometimes refers to the kingdom of heaven as the kingdom of God. They are one in the same. Now, would anyone like to read this clue?" Peg's hand bolted high into the air. "Yes, Peg, go ahead."

"And He was saying, 'The kingdom of God is like a man who casts seed on the ground; and goes to bed at night and gets up by day, and the seed sprouts up and grows - how, he himself does not know. The earth produces crops by itself; first the blade, then the head, then the mature grain in the head. But when the crop permits, he immediately puts in the sickle, because the harvest has come.'"

"Thank you, Peg. Now what could this mean? ...Any thoughts? Yes, Tom."

Tom had not been heard from yet, as a matter of fact, Tom was rarely heard from. He was the shyest boy in school and this fact caused everyone to be surprised that he would even raise his hand to offer any sort of answer. "Does...does it mean it will grow something we can use?"

*Yeah, like a new bike?* Chuck sure hoped so.

"You're right, Tom. The kingdom of God will grow something we can use. But before we go any further we are going to stop to have a treat. Does anyone like apple pie with ice cream?"

Everyone's hand rose in excitement along with a chorus of voices, "I do! I do!"

Miss Mabel dished out the homemade apple pie `a la mode then gave each child a pencil and a piece of paper. "When you are finished with your treat, I want you to write down the kind of treasures you think the kingdom of heaven should grow."

Giggles and smirks spread across the room as the children began to put down on paper the kinds of treasures they would like to harvest. The four frustrated adventurers had no problem making out their list. They had their treasures memorized from their first hunt.

When the time came to share their desires, bikes, dresses, vacations, BB guns and more where all bantered about. The children laughed at some of the wishes and tried to come up with better ones than the last one stated. Miss Mabel let them go on and on until the wish list was so big that they began to repeat what they had already wished for. Benny, though, was silent.

"Did you make out a list, Benny?" Miss Mabel saw that he had turned his piece of paper over, as if hiding what he had written. "Did you write something down? Will you share it with us?"

Benny timidly turned his paper over. There was only one thing on his list. He quietly read, "A new leg."

The room fell silent.

Miss Mabel allowed the other children time to let Benny's wish sink in and then, with a gentle spirit, spoke, "What the kingdom of heaven grows is not always the treasure we want, but I can tell you this, it is always the treasure we need... This clue from our treasure map tells us that after the man plants the seed he goes to bed by night and gets up by day. While he is doing this the seed sprouts and begins to grow. How? He does not know. But it matures and becomes something valuable enough for him to take the time to harvest, and he harvests it so that he can use it... I don't think any of you realize it yet, but a seed has been planted. Let's see what grows." Miss Mabel smiled at the children and said, "I am already looking forward to seeing you treasure hunters tomorrow."

The children slowly began to get up from their seats, lingering, almost as though they wanted to stay a little longer. Miss Mabel was at the front door, holding it open. No one spoke as they passed through.

That evening after supper, Chuck, Denny, Sam and Jess again gathered on the playground. Sam was lying on her stomach over the seat of a swing, twisting one way until the swing would twist no further then letting it untwist in the opposite direction. Chuck and Denny slowly rose up, and just as slowly dropped down on the teeter-totter. Jess was hanging by his hands on the monkey bars, swaying back and forth. Almost at once, everyone stopped.

Jess spoke first, "I sure felt bad when Benny read his list."

Chuck was wondering why he was having such a hard time letting his words out. Finally they came, "Yeah...me to."

"Benny really is a good guy... I told you he could draw, didn't I?"

Denny's friends lifted their heads and replied to him

with their eyes, *yes, you told us he could draw.*

A couple of minutes went by before Sam spoke up. "What kind of treasure do you think Miss Mabel is talking about?"

Jess was now bent down on one knee, scratching on the ground with a stick. "Beats me, but I don't think it's the kind we can buy a bike with."

"I was afraid of that." Chuck forced a half grin and then got serious, "Maybe a bike's not that important after all…"

Not one of the four friends said "see ya", they just slipped away one by one until the playground was empty.

# Chapter 9

The sun was shining, which meant Wednesday morning chores would replace gathering at the meeting place. For Jess, the chore was cutting and raking grass. He was thankful for the time alone, though, so he could think. Two days of Bible Club had left him confused. He couldn't understand why he was feeling bad about having teased Benny. Teasing had not made him feel bad before, as a matter of fact, he rather enjoyed doing it.

*This summer isn't turning out too good,* Jess thought to himself, *for a while there I figured it was going to be the best summer ever. Instead, I have no bike, and I'm feeling guilty about something I used to think was fun. I wish we could just go back to playing like we used to and forget about treasures and Bible Clubs and...and having to feel bad about something.*

Miss Mabel greeted each child by her front yard gate. Benny was the last to arrive. The big hand painted sign that read TREASURE HUNT held no promise of excitement for any of the children on this third afternoon of Bible Club. Even Peg displayed an air of glumness, not entering with her usual flair to show off her pretty dress.

"I am so happy to see all of you back here again today. I have been praying for each one of you since you left yesterday afternoon. Please open your treasure maps to Matthew 13:1-9... 'On that day Jesus went out of the house, and was sitting by the sea. And great multitudes gathered about Him, so that He got into the boat and sat down, and the whole multitude was standing on the beach. And He spoke many things to them in parables, saying, "Behold, the sower went out to sow; and as he sowed, some seeds fell beside the road, and the birds came and devoured them. And others fell upon the rocky places, where they did not have much soil; and immediately they sprang up, because they had no depth of soil. But when the sun had risen, they were scorched; and because they had no root, they withered away. And others fell among the thorns, and the thorns came up and choked them out. And others fell on good soil, and yielded a crop, some a hundredfold, some sixty, and some thirty. He who has ears, let him hear."'

"Yesterday a seed was planted," Miss Mabel smiled as she scanned the children's faces, "and you are the soil it was planted in. Today, I would like to ask...has anything grown?"

Jess avoided looking at Miss Mabel. He didn't want her asking him this question. Something had grown, but he wasn't sure what it was or how to describe it.

Miss Mabel spoke again, "Every seed sown from the kingdom of heaven is good seed."

Jess hardly realized he was thinking out loud, "It didn't feel like good seed."

"What was that, Jess?"

"Oh...I...um...I was just thinking to myself."

"What were you thinking?"

After squirming for a while, Jess decided he might just as well say what was on his mind. "Well...I felt bad when I left here yesterday, and if that was the seed that was sown...it didn't feel like a good seed to me."

"What you felt was not the seed, what you felt was because of the seed."

Jess didn't quite grasp Miss Mabel's meaning.

"Would you be willing to tell us why you felt so bad?"

Jess stared at the ground. A couple of days earlier he would not have even considered answering a question like this, but today he seemed to be struggling to keep words in that were fighting to get out. Finally, he blurted, "I...I've been a bully to Benny. I've teased and made fun of him for a long time."

When Jess didn't go on, Miss Mabel asked, "Did you

know it was wrong?"

"...At first I guess I did, but...after teasing him for so long I didn't feel bad about it anymore. Everyone was doing it...so...I didn't think I was so bad for doing it too."

"Why do you feel bad about it now?"

"I don't know." Jess shifted in his seat and wished Miss Mabel's questions would stop. After about thirty seconds of trying to figure out a way not to answer, he decided to jump back in. "Yesterday, when we were reading our lists...mine was all about fun things: a bike, a hockey stick, skates." Jess became very solemn... "Things I knew Benny couldn't do. When he read his list...well, like Chuck said last night, maybe a bike isn't so important after all. Shoot," Jess looked up to expose a tear running down his cheek, "I wanted all these toys, and Benny just wanted to be able to walk." Turning to the boy he had antagonized for so long, Jess said, "I'm sorry, Benny. I won't blame you if you can't forgive me... I've been really rotten to you."

Benny wanted to say, *that's OK, I forgive you,* but he couldn't. He had something of his own that he needed to deal with. "I'm sorry too, Jess."

Jess looked surprised. "For what? You didn't do anything wrong."

"Yes I did. I hated you... I hated you more than I hated

anybody... I...I think I might still hate you...but I don't want to anymore."

All eyes where fixed on Benny. Most of them knew that at one time or another they also had been guilty of teasing. Chuck's heart was pounding and his face felt as hot as burning coal. He knew what he had to do, but was having a hard time making his feet move. Mustering up courage, he stood from his chair and walked over to face his victim. "I've bullied you too, and I'm sorry." Benny was now in tears. Chuck pointed to the empty chair next to him and asked, "Can I sit here?"

Benny wiped his wet cheeks with his shirt sleeve, "...Sure."

Before long, all the children realized they had some business to take care of. Denny confessed his guilt of going along with Jess and Chuck instead of being Benny's friend. Sam apologized to Peg for all the bad things she had said about her behind her back. Peg apologized to Sam and the other girls for having worked as hard as she did to try and make them jealous. And on it went.

Miss Mabel left the children alone for a short time to talk things out, but soon returned with a tray full of ice cream sundae fixings. "Come and make yourselves a sundae, and as you're doing so I'll share some thoughts with you.

"I want to show you where you can find the description of the seed that was sown yesterday. I will read it for you out of my treasure map. A man asked Jesus what the greatest commandment of the law was and Jesus' answer is recorded in Matthew 22:37-39, '...You shall love the Lord your God with all your heart, and with all your soul, and with all your mind. This is the great and foremost commandment. And the second is like it, you shall love your neighbor as yourself.' The seed that was sown was this second greatest commandment, love for others, and judging by the fruit it has borne...it has fallen on good soil.

"Jess, I told you that your feeling bad was not the seed, but rather because of the seed. As Samantha pointed out on Monday, the kingdom of heaven causes change...from the inside out...like the yeast causes bread to rise. This seed of love for others from the kingdom has grown into a love for Benny, and that love has shed light on your guilt. We are beginning to get a glimpse of the kind of treasure the kingdom of heaven has to offer.

"You also learned something very important today. You learned that gaining new treasure can come at a cost. You gave something up to acquire the treasure you found. Bullying, jealousy, hate; they can not live side by side with love for others. You relinquished former treasures,

treasures you enjoyed even though they were destroying you on the inside, to acquire a treasure of greater value. As you go to bed tonight, think on these things and decide if you would like to keep hunting, because the treasure we are yet to find is of far greater value…and it comes at a far greater cost."

Six friends gathered on the playground after supper. Jess pushed Benny on the swing as the girls spun on the merry-go-round. Peg wasn't worried about her dress because she was wearing an old pair of pedal pushers, and Sam was thinking maybe she would go to one of Peg's tea parties if she ever invited her. Chuck and Denny were on the teeter-totter once again, pushing hard and laughing.

## GRANDDAD'S STORY

# Chapter 10

Thursday's Bible Club began early, as all the children had arrived fifteen minutes ahead of time. The glumness of the day before had been replaced by anticipation.

"We have witnessed first hand how something from the kingdom of heaven affects our everyday lives." Miss Mabel was overjoyed by the children's eagerness to hunt on.

"Miss Mabel?"

"Yes, Samantha."

"Just what is the kingdom of heaven?"

"It is where God reigns."

"How do we get there?"

"By leaving this world behind."

"You mean...when we die?"

"I mean when we live...forever!"

The children began looking at each other as if to say, *what on earth is Miss Mabel talking about now?*

"There is a gate that you must enter to get into the kingdom of heaven."

The wheels of Jess' imagination began to turn, "Just

one gate?"

"Yes."

"Is it a magic gate?"

"A magic gate? Oh for goodness sakes no, but it is a narrow gate. Why don't you all pick up your treasure maps and turn to Matthew 7: 13-14. Is there anyone who is willing to read this for us?"

Chuck raised his hand before he even found the verses. "'Enter by the narrow gate; for the gate is wide, and the way is broad that leads to destruction, and many are those who enter by it. For the gate is small, and the way is narrow that leads to life, and few are those who find it.' It sounds like there are two gates."

"Yes, but only one leads to life. Where does the other gate lead to?"

Chuck looked over the verses again, "To destruction."

Miss Mabel turned her attention back to all the children, "That's right, destruction. We only have to revisit yesterday to understand that we had already known about the wide gate. Jess, what did you give up yesterday that was destructive?"

Jess was embarrassed to even say the words, "…being a bully."

"Peg, how about you?"

"Trying to make the other girls jealous."

"And, Benny?"

Benny's answer was slow in coming. It hurt to be reminded of how he had felt about Jess, "...Hate."

"Those were all destructive, and they all came from the wide gate. Love for others has come from the narrow gate. Was it easier to bully, try to make people jealous, hate...or was it easier to love others?"

Chuck thought this might be a trick question. He was sure Miss Mabel wanted them to answer "love others", but, for him, that was the hardest thing to do. He decided to let someone else take a shot at answering.

Benny, very quietly said, "To hate."

"Yes, it is easier to hate someone than to love someone. Why do you suppose that is?"

No one ventured to answer this question.

"It is because when we hate someone, we put ourselves first. When we truly love someone we put that person ahead of ourselves. Chuck, when you walked over to Benny yesterday and apologized, was it easy? Wouldn't it have been easier to stay in your chair and say nothing?" Miss Mabel went on before Chuck could reply. "We know the answer. We saw how hard it was for you. You weighed your discomfort against the discomfort you saw in Benny, and you decided you cared more about his discomfort than you did about your own. You put Benny first, before yourself."

"Does...does that mean I'm in the kingdom of heaven?" Chuck was hoping he had found the treasure before the others.

"No." Miss Mabel looked at him with sadness, "You are much too dirty to be in the kingdom of heaven. Remember, this is where God reigns. He would not allow you in His presence as dirty as you are."

Chuck was visibly shaken by Miss Mabel's comment. He tried to understand what she could possibly mean. He looked at his hands and clothes. He thought, *is my face dirty?* He had taken a bath last night. He even combed his hair and brushed his teeth before he came to Bible Club.

"I see what you are thinking, Chuck, but that is not the kind of dirt I am talking about. It is the lack of cleanliness in your heart that is the problem."

Chuck immediately remembered how selfish he had been with his new bike. Not once had he let any of his three best friends ride it. He kept it all to himself, not willing to share. Then he remembered what he had said under his breath to his mom a few days earlier, something he would never dare say to her face. One thing after another ran through his mind, things he was now ashamed of.

"All of us are too dirty to stand in the presence of God, and yet God wants every one of us to enter into His kingdom. The gate which leads to life is narrow for a reason. The reason is that we cannot take anything with us. If we try to enter the narrow gate clinging to our possessions...hate, selfishness, jealousy...we won't fit. The gate is not wide enough for us to take the possessions of our heart. We must be willing to give up our possessions and enter with nothing."

Chuck was thinking hard now. *Everything? Even the good things?* "Miss Mabel?"

"Yes, Chuck."

"When you say everything, are you talking about just the things in our heart or everything we own?"

"Everything you own is in your heart, Chuck."

*Huh? Everything I own is in my heart?* Chuck's hand went to the back of his head and began to scratch. *I've got to be missing something here.* "What if I got a new bike and I was willing to share it with my friends? That would be a good thing. If I wasn't selfish with it, couldn't I have that in the kingdom of heaven?"

"Nothing will fit through the gate, Chuck, except you."

Jess was beginning to wonder if there was a down side to the kingdom of heaven. Giving up bullying is one thing, but giving up everything you have is a lot to ask.

Chuck continued, "I don't get it. How can the things I have be in my heart?"

"Yesterday I ended Bible Club by asking you to decide if you want to keep on hunting because the treasure we have yet to find will come at a far greater cost. This is the cost; that you are willing to give up everything for the treasure of far greater value."

There was stillness in the air. Every child at Bible Club was mentally running through the list of their possessions.

"When our possessions hold greater value than being in the presence of God, we are worshiping idols over God. That worship comes from the heart. God tells us in Exodus 20:3, 'You shall have no other Gods before Me.'"

"That's what makes us dirty, isn't it." Sam's confession spoke of what was in her own heart. She had heard many times in Sunday School about sin, but never really understood her own sin. "Miss Mabel," Sam's eyes began to fill with tears, "If we're so dirty...how can we ever get into the kingdom of heaven?"

"We can enter because, '...God so loved the world, that He gave His only begotten Son, that whoever believes in Him should not perish, but have eternal life. For God did not send the Son into the world to judge the world; but that the world should be saved through Him.'

"This statement was made by Jesus. We find it in our treasure maps in John 3:16-17. Jesus was speaking of Himself. In John 14:6 He says, '...I am the way, the truth, and the life; no one comes to the Father, but through Me.' The Father sent Jesus into the world to provide the way for us to enter the kingdom of heaven. He provides the way for us to stand clean before the Father."

Miss Mabel knew she needed to explain. "Samantha, if you were caught in the act of stealing candy from the candy store, do you think the storekeeper would welcome you the next time you wanted to enter his shop?"

"I don't think he would."

"You are right. He would not. In his eyes you would be stained with the reputation of a thief. And what could you do that would change how he sees you so that you would once again be welcome?"

"Tell him I'm sorry for stealing the candy."

"Oh, there is much more that is required. He needs to see the brokenness of your heart. He needs to know you understand the seriousness of the crime. The stain of a thief is not washed away by a mere apology, it is washed away by a repentant heart and the payment of the debt owed."

Miss Mabel addressed all the children. "Sin is the breaking of God's law. God, who is righteous and holy, sees the stain of our guilt. When we steal, He sees the stain of a thief. When we lie, He sees the stain of a liar. When we are selfish, He sees the stain of selfishness. We cannot enter into His presence stained as we are. But He loves us and wants us in His presence. God has sent His one and only Son, Jesus, to the earth for the sole purpose of providing the way for us to stand in His presence.

"We cannot clean the stain of sin from our souls, for the stain is much too deep. We cannot pay the debt of sin owed, for the debt is far too great. Jesus lived the life of a perfect man and therefore had the right to offer Himself as the payment for our sin. He did this by allowing Himself to be put to death on a cross. You may not fully understand now, but as you study God's word you will see that the stain of our sin is washed clean by the blood Jesus shed on that cross. He is the way. He is the gate. Our Heavenly Father sees us without stain or blemish as we enter the kingdom through His Son.

"Jesus is the pearl of great value. He is the treasure hidden in the field for which the farmer is willing to sell all of his possessions. Isaiah 53:5-6 tells us that, '...He was pierced through for our transgressions, He was crushed for our iniquities; The chastening for our well-being fell upon Him, and by His scourging we are healed. All of us like sheep have gone astray, each of us has turned to his own way; But the Lord has caused the iniquity of us all to fall on Him.' ...And He has done this out of love for us, for He tells us in John 15:13, 'Greater love has no one than this, that one lay done his life for his friends.'"

Miss Mabel stopped, giving the children time to consider all she had said. Then she went on, "I want you to know that it didn't end there. Jesus did die, but He did not stay in the grave. He conquered death and walked out of the grave, proving His authority to offer us eternal life. Death is not just having these bodies we live in die, death is eternal separation from God. Jesus is offering us the way to be saved from death and in doing so we will live forever with Him. We are told in Romans 10:9-10, '...that if you confess with your mouth Jesus as Lord, and believe in your heart that God raised Him from the dead, you shall be saved; for with the heart man believes, resulting in righteousness, and with the mouth he confesses, resulting in salvation.'

"Think about what you have heard. Jesus is offering to wash your sins away. The debt has already been paid. Is the value of the treasure of Jesus far greater than the value of the treasures you now possess? Answering this question is unavoidable, for John 3:18 tells us, 'He who believes in Him is not judged; he who does not believe has been judged already, because he has not believed in the name of the only begotten Son of God.' In other words, if you have not accepted Jesus, you have already rejected Jesus.

"You may take your treasure maps home with you today, they are my gift to you, but please remember to bring them to Bible Club tomorrow." Miss Mabel folded her hands on her lap, "I have been praying for each one of you every day. Today I will be praying that God draws your hearts to Him, that you desire to know Him and to live in His kingdom." The Bible Club afternoon ended with Miss Mabel's renowned triple fudge brownies...and lots of questions about Jesus.

The playground was fast becoming the new meeting place. Six friends now gathered in the evening. Everyone but Jess wanted to talk about the things Miss Mabel had told them.

Sam was the first to speak up, "Miss Mabel sure has me thinking."

"About what?" Denny knew, for he was thinking the same thing, but didn't really want to say it out loud.

"About Jesus."

Chuck chimed in, "Yeah, me too."

Jess couldn't stop thinking about all that talk of giving

up everything he owned for Jesus. "Hey! Anybody want to play pirates in the morning? We can pretend they are climbing the hill and we can jump the wall and drive them back down to the river!" Jess thought it might be good to think about something else for a while.

"Jess!" Chuck allowed his expression to finish his sentence, *we can't do that.* Then he tilted his head toward Benny.

Jess stared at Benny for a few seconds and then dropped his eyes; *nothing will be the same now.*

## GRANDDAD'S STORY

# Chapter 11

The last afternoon of Bible Club arrived sooner than Jess had wanted. He was sure Miss Mabel was going to ask if anyone was ready to enter the kingdom of heaven. He was not. The more he thought over the past week, the more he wanted things to be the way they were. He was OK with being friends with Benny and he knew that he didn't want to be a bully any more, but he was afraid of what else might change. He liked wanting to have a new bike and wanting to buy model cars to build. He liked the way things had been with his friends, and he was a little angry that having new friends would change how he could play with his old friends.

Miss Mabel opened Bible Club by confirming every fear Jess had. "I must warn you, that one lives in the kingdom of heaven differently than one lives in the world. When you enter the kingdom of heaven through Jesus you will not remain the same. We are told in Ephesians 5:1-2, 'Therefore be imitators of God, as beloved children; and walk in love, just as Christ also loved you, and gave Himself up for us, an offering and a sacrifice to God as a fragrant aroma.' This is not easy to do. It requires us to let go of our old life and live a new life in Jesus, who is the Christ. But, as we have already seen, the transformation from old to new only hurts for a short time."

Miss Mabel rose from her chair, walked into the house, and returned with a full tray of lemonade and cookies. As she offered some to each child she asked, "Chuck, remember what it felt like when you sat in your chair the other day, deciding whether or not you should ask Benny to forgive you?"

"I sure do."

"Did it hurt?"

"Yes, it hurt bad."

"How does it feel now?"

Chuck was sitting next to Benny, he put his arm around Benny's shoulders, smiled and said, "It feels good...real good."

"So you see, the pain of giving up the things that are leading to our destruction is replaced by the joy of what God grows in its absence."

Jess could not argue with this. He didn't know last week, but he did know now, that he would much rather be Benny's friend than his bully. "Miss Mabel, what if I want..."

"Ah! There is the problem."

Jess was startled. "The problem?"

"Yes, the problem. I know, because you have not entered the kingdom of heaven yet, that your 'I want' is the problem. If you are considering giving your life to Jesus, who is the Christ, the One who gave His life for yours, you are afraid that you will have to give up all your wants and desires, and you are right…you will. But that's not to say that all of your wants and desires are bad, they are only bad if you are not willing to give them up for Christ.

"Jess, Jesus loves you. The first thing He wants from you is your heart. If you are willing to give that to Him He will take very good care of it. He will gently, over time, transform those wants and desires to become the same as His wants and desires. You will not stop living life. You will live life to the fullest. Jesus tells us in John 10:10, '…I came that they might have life, and might have it abundantly.' That means to the full, more life than you can imagine. The problem is, before we know Jesus as our Savior we do not see life in the same way that He does. When we are lost in the world, having entered through the wide gate, we only see what the world has to offer. We believe that this is what life is. But when we step through the narrow gate, enter into new life through Christ, we are introduced to the truth of life and are overwhelmed by its fullness.

"Children, God will not force you to give up anything that you have, but your unwillingness to give something to Him will block your ability to receive what He wants you to have in its place. Simply put, you can not step into new life if you are unwilling to step out of the old life.

"I have one more scripture I want to share with you. It is found in Matthew 6:19-21. 'Do not lay up for yourselves treasures upon earth, where moth and rust destroy, and where thieves break in and steal. But lay up for yourselves treasures in heaven, where neither moth nor rust destroys, and where thieves do not break in and steal; for where your treasure is, there will your heart be also.'"

Miss Mabel's voice faded behind thoughts that rushed into the minds of four very close friends. Sam, Denny, Chuck, and Jess slowly began to look at each other in astonishment, each remembering Chuck's bike being stolen, Jess' bike rusting away, and the moth eaten map. Their hearts began to ache. They remembered the selfish desire that possessed them in their drive to find what they thought would make them rich. They remembered their anger when they realized their best adventure ever had come to an abrupt end.

Without their knowledge God had planned a different adventure for them, the GREATEST adventure ever...the one that led to eternal life.

~~~

Granddad smiled broadly at his grandchildren. "Yes! We found our treasure! It wasn't the treasure we expected to find when we first began our hunt…no…it was a treasure of far, far greater value. It was the pearl of GREAT value. And how did our treasure affect our lives? It changed us completely from the inside out. Not all at once mind you, but over time. We studied God's word together and experienced the excitement of having many seeds from the kingdom of heaven sown into our soil.

"A seed called forgiveness was planted, grew and was harvested very early in Chuck's new life. At the end of the summer his stolen bike was returned to him. The thief was a young boy from a very poor family. He knew he couldn't bring the bike home because his parents would want to know where the bike had come from, so he kept it hidden in the woods and took it out to ride when no one was around. After a while his guilt got the better of him, and his secret joy lost its luster. He confessed to his parents what he had done. He was punished and was made to bring the bike back to Chuck and tell him the whole truth.

"We had been studying the Lord's Prayer with Miss Mabel the week this took place. There is a line in the prayer that asks God to forgive us of our sins in the way we forgive those who sin against us. Chuck knew his own heart and understood how much he needed to be forgiven by God. In light of this, his anger against the thief was gone. He thanked the boy, who was only eight years old, for telling him the truth and for returning his bike. On Christmas morning of that year Chuck tied a big red bow on his bike, took it to the boy's house, and left it at his front door. He attached a Christmas card to the handlebar on which he had written these words: 'Ricky, please let me give this to you. I want you to know that I really do forgive you and that you mean more to me than my bike does. And I want to tell you about Jesus. He forgave me for the things I've done wrong. He will forgive you too. Merry Christmas! Your friend, Chuck.'

"Yes, the treasure of Jesus has affected our whole lives. He has changed our dreams, our desires. We fell in love with His word, the Bible, and studied it together until we graduated from high school. Sam went on to become a doctor and Peg a nurse. Both have given their lives to sharing their medical skills and the gospel throughout small villages in Africa. Denny studied art and gives glory to his Lord by making scriptural accounts come alive on canvas. Chuck went into banking. He has a ministry on the side that teaches people how to be wise in the use of their money. Benny became a professor at a Bible College, a professor who says he will not retire as long as there are young people who desire to 'hunt for treasure'. And me? Well, you know what happened to me. I became a Granddad with the most wonderful ministry of all. I get to share the good news of the gospel of Jesus Christ with my grandchildren in hopes that you, too, will embark on your GREATEST adventure ever!"